D0102874

Dear Parents:

Congratulations! Your child is taking the first steps on an exciting journey. The destination? Independent reading!

STEP INTO READING® will help your child get there. The program offers five steps to reading success. Each step includes fun stories and colorful art or photographs. In addition to original fiction and books with favorite characters, there are Step into Reading Non-Fiction Readers, Phonics Readers and Boxed Sets, Sticker Readers, and Comic Readers—a complete literacy program with something to interest every child.

Learning to Read, Step by Step!

Ready to Read **Preschool–Kindergarten**
• big type and easy words • rhyme and rhythm • picture clues
For children who know the alphabet and are eager to begin reading.

Reading with Help **Preschool–Grade 1**
• basic vocabulary • short sentences • simple stories
For children who recognize familiar words and sound out new words with help.

Reading on Your Own **Grades 1–3**
• engaging characters • easy-to-follow plots • popular topics
For children who are ready to read on their own.

Reading Paragraphs **Grades 2–3**
• challenging vocabulary • short paragraphs • exciting stories
For newly independent readers who read simple sentences with confidence.

Ready for Chapters **Grades 2–4**
• chapters • longer paragraphs • full-color art
For children who want to take the plunge into chapter books but still like colorful pictures.

STEP INTO READING® is designed to give every child a successful reading experience. The grade levels are only guides; children will progress through the steps at their own speed, developing confidence in their reading.

Remember, a lifetime love of reading starts with a single step!

© 2018 Spin Master Ltd. All rights reserved. Published in the United States by Random House Children's Books, a division of Penguin Random House LLC, 1745 Broadway, New York, NY 10019, and in Canada by Penguin Random House Canada Limited, Toronto. Rusty Rivets and all related titles, logos, and characters are trademarks of Spin Master Ltd. Nickelodeon, Nick Jr., and all related titles and logos are trademarks of Viacom International Inc.

Step into Reading, Random House, and the Random House colophon are registered trademarks of Penguin Random House LLC.

Visit us on the Web!
StepIntoReading.com
rhcbooks.com

Educators and librarians, for a variety of teaching tools, visit us at RHTeachersLibrarians.com

ISBN 978-1-5247-7273-4 (trade) — ISBN 978-1-5247-7274-1 (lib. bdg.)

Printed in the United States of America

10 9 8 7 6 5 4 3 2 1

Random House Children's Books supports the First Amendment and celebrates the right to read.

THE GREAT MONKEY SHOW!

adapted by Delphine Finnegan

based on the teleplay
"Monkey Mayhem" by Ron Holsey

illustrated by Donald Cassity

Random House New York

Rusty and Ruby
visit the Animal Park.
They want to see
the monkey show!

Ranger Anna
has a problem.
The monkeys are bored.
They will not perform.

Ruby has an idea.

She and Rusty

will create a new act!

Ranger Anna leaves
to feed the seals.
Rusty and Ruby stay
with the monkeys.

Rusty and Ruby
try to think
of a new act
for the monkeys.

But they have a problem.

The monkeys escape!

Rusty and Ruby follow them into town. They find the monkeys juggling apples.

The monkeys run away!
They take Rusty's go-kart
and Ruby's buggy.

They take Officer Carl's hovercycle, too!

Rusty and Ruby
chase the monkeys.
They find them
in the park.

The monkeys
spin and flip.
They climb up high.

At the ice cream shop,
the monkeys bang drums
and dance to the beat.

Rusty and Ruby
have a great idea
for the monkeys' new act!

Rusty, Ruby, and
the Bits get to work.
The monkeys help.

They make the
Drum-o-matic Monkey-tastic
Showstopper 5000!
Soon it is time for
the show.

The monkeys juggle.
They bang on the drums.
They love the
new invention!

The crowd claps and cheers for the monkeys.

Everyone loves
their new act!

The great monkey show is a hit, thanks to Rusty, Ruby, and the Bits!